THE DESERTED GROOM

MAIL ORDER BRIDES OF CULVER'S CREEK

SUSANNAH CALLOWAY

Tica House
Publishing

Sweet Romance that Delights and Enchants!

PERSONAL WORD FROM THE AUTHOR

Dearest Readers,

Thank you so much for choosing one of my books. I am proud to be a part of the team of writers at Tica House Publishing who work joyfully to bring you stories of hope, faith, courage, and love. Your kind words and loving readership are deeply appreciated.

I would like to personally invite you to sign up for updates and to become part of our **Exclusive Reader Club**—it's completely Free to join! We'd love to welcome you!

Much love,

Susannah Calloway

VISIT HERE to Join our Reader's Club and to Receive Tica House Updates!

https://wesrom.subscribemenow.com/

CONTENTS

CHAPTER 1

The first light dusting of snow was beginning to accumulate on the steps outside as the bride came down the aisle, a small bouquet of the last few black-eyed Susans in her hands. She was dressed in her mother's wedding gown, a gesture that was not to be overlooked in the small town of Culver's Creek, Missouri, steeped in tradition as it was. The veil was new, though; ordered special through the mercantile. In the marriage of his youngest daughter, the last to leave the house, Martin Connor was prepared to spare no expense.

The last of the daughters to leave the house, at least. The oldest of the four Connor siblings, and the only boy, stood with his mother in the second aisle, watching his youngest sister proceed past the gamut of admiring gazes. Martin let his eyes rest on the young man, feeling the familiar tug at his heart. His only son, the man who would inherit the ranch and carry on the family name. Martin loved all his children, but Val had a special spot in his heart. He could only hope that it wasn't as obvious to all as he feared it was.

He sighed, turning his gaze back to Lydia. She was just eighteen, and every inch the sweetest, prettiest bride Culver's Creek had ever seen – at least, since her two sisters got married. Yes, he was proud of all his children. If they could all see the same sort of happiness that was on Lydia's beaming face right this moment, he would go to his grave content.

His wife tucked her arm through his, stepping closer. She gave him a teary-eyed smile, her face filled with fondness and love, and he put a hand over hers, pressing warmly. His heart swelled with the happiness of the occasion – and, faintly, his fear for the future. He tried his best to push the thought away. There was no use borrowing trouble…

Martin resisted the urge to press a kiss to his wife's temple. It wasn't that the townsfolk in Culver's Creek would frown on such a public display of affection between an old married man and his wife, exactly – but he had something of a reputation to uphold in this town, even now.

He did allow himself to lean closer and whisper into her ear.

"You're as pretty as the day I married you, Bernice."

Though she nudged him and murmured, "Oh, please," as though his words were ridiculous, he could tell that she appreciated them all the same by the blush that stole over her cheeks. Yes, his daughters had come by their rosy-cheeked, golden-haired looks honestly, inheriting them from their mother. Val, now – Val had a different sort of look to him. Tall of form and narrow of feature, with dark hair and black eyes, and there was such an intensity to everything he did. Martin could only think that his son had inherited it from further back on the line, some grandparent who came over from Italy in the cargo hold of a tempest-tossed ship...

Passionate, that was the word for Val, and it was only the careful raising by his parents that kept him from being hot-tempered. A boy like that – a man, Martin reminded himself quickly, though he couldn't help but persist in thinking of his children as, well, children – a man like that, with energies like his, would easily make some sweet girl the best husband in all of Culver's Creek.

If only his options weren't so very...limited.

He couldn't help but wonder what his son was thinking now. Those thick black brows were drawn closely down over the bridge of his nose, and he looked as though he were concentrating – but not on the marriage of his sister, for his eyes were diverted from the couple at the front of the chapel. No, he was thinking of something else – or trying to avoid it.

Martin had a feeling that he knew what it was.

The ceremony was ending, and Martin realized with a start that his brooding over his son's future had kept him from paying much attention to his youngest daughter's wedding. A wave of guilt washed over him, and he turned his gaze to the happy couple, clapping dutifully as they were announced as husband and wife to the assembled throng. Well, there they had it – Lydia Connor no more, but Lydia Halstrom, and now there were no more little daughters to chat and giggle in the sprawling ranch house on the Connor acreage.

The faint pulse of sadness that sounded deep in his heart must have shown on his face, for his wife turned to him and put a hand on his cheek.

"She's the happiest I've ever seen her," she whispered. "And Lyle will take good care of her."

Martin nodded.

"He'd better," he said, though he meant it jokingly – more or less.

They followed the triumphant couple out into the weak gray light of early autumn, and applauded as Lyle Halstrom handed his new bride up into the waiting carriage. The newlyweds rode off into the flurry of tiny snowflakes, and once again Bernice slid her hands around Martin's arm, smiling up at him.

"Well," she said, "that couldn't have gone better. What a lovely ceremony."

Martin nodded, his eyes on the young women who were hurrying toward them. "And here come your daughters to tell you all about why theirs was better," he said.

Bernice laughed and pushed him away lightly.

"Go on with you. Each wedding is the most beautiful, and I won't hear anyone tell me any different."

"You'd better let them know that, then."

Bernice sighed happily.

"There's just something so – so very beautiful about a marriage of two people who truly love each other, don't you think, Martin?"

"I think you're a romantic at heart, Bernice – too romantic for your own good, I reckon."

"How you do like to tease me, Martin." She pinched his cheek, smiling up at him. "What on earth will I do with you?"

She went to meet her daughters and their husbands, and Martin caught sight of Val standing off to himself, hands in his pockets. His son gave him a faint smile as he approached, but it was still clear that his thoughts were elsewhere.

"Well, son, what do you make of it?"

Val took his hands from his pockets respectfully, rubbing the back of his neck.

"That's been three weddings in two years, Pa," he said. "The rate you're going, you're either going to run out of children to marry off or money to pay the preacher. And I have a feeling I know which one will come first."

Martin gave him a smile, and after a moment, Val returned it. A stronger smile this time, though his eyes were still far away.

"Fancy a big church wedding like this yourself, eh?"

A cloud passed over his son's dark eyes, and Val turned away.

"Don't reckon it matters much anymore what I want, does it?"

Martin took a deep breath. Martin Percival Connor – twenty-six years old, handsome enough to make any girl cry into her pillow, with a strong spirit and a good head for business, and his whole life ahead of him. To hear the bitterness in his tone was enough to make his father's heart falter, even if it had not already been in difficulties.

How to explain to his only son the fears that had taken root in his troubled heart? The shortness of his breath, the way some mornings it felt like the devil himself was sitting on his chest – and the last fear, the biggest fear, the one that kept him up at night. That he would die without making the final arrangements for the care of his beloved wife. That Val would spend his life waiting for Linda Mallory to come back to him, and never father any children to pass on the family name – and the ranch. That the Connor acreage would pass, instead, into the hands of creditors and bankers who already had seen fit to remind Martin of his debt, even on the day of his daughter's wedding.

He knew it was his own doing, mostly. There had been a few bad years – nothing that they couldn't handle, in the grander scheme of things. The Lord knew that Connor Ranch had seen its fair share of lean times when the children were little. But then came the trouble with Val and Linda Mallory; then came the need to pay for the weddings of all three of his girls, one after another. And then came the pain in his chest...he knew that doctors' visits weren't far off, if he wanted to survive as long as he could.

And he did. Martin Connor loved life; he loved his family, his farm, and above all his beloved wife. He wasn't about to let some little failure of the heart get in the way.

In the back of his mind, the thought lurked: even the famous Connor stubbornness could not cure a failing heart.

He cleared his throat, letting the seriousness of his thoughts come forth in his tone.

"Well, son," he said. "We'd better sit down and have a conversation about all that, tonight. I've got some...news for you."

His son turned his large dark eyes on him, full of curiosity, but Martin shook his head, managing another smile. A smile that, he suspected, Val could see straight through, for his lips firmed in a stern line, and his brows drew down once more.

"It's your sister's wedding day," Martin told him, putting a hand on his shoulder. "Let's just concentrate on that, eh? There'll be time soon enough to talk of other things."

And even if Val urged him to spill his secrets, then and there, he was determined that he would not let himself be prevailed upon to say another word.

But Val did no urging; he did not try to prevail on his father. Instead, with that closed-off look still on his face, he only nodded unhappily and turned his eyes back toward the joyous throng that always attended in the wake of a wedding.

That was how Martin knew that his instincts had been correct.

Something had to give.

And Val Connor, like it or not, had to forget about his love and move on.

CHAPTER 2

His sister's wedding day.

Hard to wrap his mind around the fact that there had been three such occasions in just under two years; even harder to realize that it was Lydia, this time, who was saying goodbye to the house they had all grown up in. It was going to be a great deal quieter around the ranch, Val reflected with a rueful grin; his sisters had filled every room with endless chatter, and he had been their favorite target. The oldest of the bunch, the only brother, and the target for alternating teasing and lectures. Well, they all had their husbands to tease and lecture now.

He, on the other hand, had nothing but a quiet house, his aging parents, and the running of the ranch to attend to.

And that, he was becoming convinced, was all he would ever have.

Not a day went by that he didn't think of Linda. He shied away from the thoughts, but they presented themselves again and again, regardless. They had really only known each other for a few months, but that was more than enough for him to fall head over heels. He knew himself to be quick-minded, making decisions on the spur of the moment. He had decided to marry Linda almost from the moment he first saw her.

She was Timothy Barrow's niece, visiting her relatives from out of county. Some little town up in northern Missouri; far enough away that Val had never heard of it, and far enough away to lend Linda a sort of exotic aura. She was as dark-haired as he was himself, but her eyes were a pale sky blue, a striking contrast. She was shy, he decided when she hardly spoke in response to his questions, but shyness was no bad thing in such a young woman. Indeed, it was almost a virtue, compared to the loudly outgoing nature of his sisters.

For the first month that she had been in town, he had sought out every chance to be near her, to get to know her. There were few unmarried women in Culver's Creek – at the time, three of them had been his sisters. He was twenty-four then and had watched most of his friends marry and start families. Every little inkling of romance in his soul had settled on the person of Linda Mallory.

And she had seemed to accept his advances. Shy though she was, she certainly smiled at him a great deal, and let him sit with her at every supper and gathering in town. Later, she let him hold her hand. And the final month before she had left to go back up north to her mother's house, she had agreed with a quiet smile to become his bride.

Val closed his eyes now, blotting out the sight of the wedding party, and wishing he could blot out the memory of his own rapture when his proposal was accepted. No, she had not been ecstatic, but in a quiet, refined girl like Linda, a showy display would have been out of place. She had given him her staid, quiet smile and said yes to the most important question he could ever ask, and that was enough to light up Val's life for the rest of his days.

Or so he had thought.

Arrangements had been made. She would return home and tell her mother of her engagement; her father had died some years before, and so Val had spoken to her uncle Timothy in lieu of asking permission of her parents. Permission had been granted swiftly; the Connors were a respectable, well-liked family, even if they were not the richest folks in Missouri. Once home, Linda would pack her things, say goodbye to her friends, and travel south again a month later to marry Val and begin their lives together.

A month came and went, and there was no sign of Linda.

Val wrote to her faithfully. At first, there were a few letters, excusing her without giving an explanation. A month, two months, six months. Then, gradually, silence. He went to Timothy Barrow, and was told that he'd heard nothing either. There was no news; there was nothing to tell. All Tim could tell him was that no tragic accident had befallen the family; he knew nothing more. A year went by, and Val knew that he should give her up. Something had changed, and he didn't know what; not knowing was driving him wild. He took a train north to the little town where she was from, but no one there would tell him where she lived.

Every now and then, when he least expected it, a letter would arrive, brief and hurried, with no excuses or reasons or even professions of undying adoration, but just enough to remind him of their engagement and to fan the flames of his love.

But now – now, it had been six months since the last one, and the love in his heart had solidified into a stone-like bitterness.

Love, he thought, is not always what you think it will be. He opened his eyes again and looked about himself at the wedding party. The cake had been cut, and there were a handful of couples dancing a reel in the middle of the dancing floor. The air was full of the sound of joyousness, of celebration. But what was the point of it all? What was the point of falling in love with someone who could walk away so easily, and disappear, seemingly forever?

At least the party was, at last, ending. It had been little short of torture for him from beginning to end. Even during the ceremony, all he had been able to think was how lovely Linda would have looked in her wedding dress, how much he longed to stand before the preacher with the woman he loved, take her by the hand and promise his life to her...

Why had his love gone so wrong when his sisters' marriages had been so blessed?

His soul was in a turmoil of anger, anguish, and guilt. Somehow, perhaps, he had done something, said something that made Linda leave him and run away...

But then, if so...why the letters she had sent?

It made no sense, and his mind was exhausted from thinking it over and trying to force it into some semblance of logic. The only relief that he found in the moment was to look to where his parents stood in the corner, near the punch bowl. He couldn't help but smile at the sight of them. This, he knew, was what true love looked like. The two of them, growing old together, and still with that glint, that spark in their eyes when they looked at each other. His mother's hair was entirely gray now, but her face still looked as youthful as it had a decade before. His father had grown thin recently – rather haggard, Val realized suddenly with a faint frown. But he still carried himself with a vital demeanor, and he still oversaw every aspect of the ranch, reluctant yet to hand any of them off to his son.

Though he would have to, in the end – Val was the only inheritor, and he couldn't quite understand why his father was so reluctant to allow him more insight into the inner workings of the ranch. Why, if he knew the state of the finances, he could arrange to purchase more acres, to sell cattle to clients further away, to rebuild the old barn that had half fallen in the last year and double their stable capacity...

Be patient, Percival Connor, he chided himself sternly. It's Pa's ranch, not yours. Not yet. And he loves it with all his heart and soul. So, you just be patient.

After all, it wasn't just his looks or his stubbornness that he had inherited from his father, but his great love of the family, too.

He wondered idly what his father had to say to him, what was so important that he couldn't just spill the beans then and there at the wedding.

He found out soon enough.

After the celebrations were over, the last goodbyes had been said, and the three remaining Connors had returned to the ranch house, they sat for a few minutes together in the kitchen, discussing the day in quiet tones. Val could see the exhaustion on his mother's face, but it was a satisfied sort of tiredness. She had married off her last daughter and had only her son to plan for now. Marrying off a son was a very different matter than arranging a daughter's wedding, after all – boys were so much less likely to kick up a fuss about flowers and such things. At least, that was how Bernice Connor had put it earlier, and it made Val smile even while his heart winced. Would his mother ever get the chance to see her son happily wed? The more time that passed, the more bitter he grew, the less likely it seemed.

His father was equally exhausted, but there was a haunted look in his eyes, rather than satisfaction. He was thinking, Val surmised, about the upcoming interview between the two of them. The thought made his heart sink, his courage falter. Whatever it was that his father had to tell him, it was far from good news.

"Well, that's it for me," Bernice said at last, sipping the last bit of her tea and standing up. "I reckon we'll all sleep better tonight, with the hubbub over and Lydia settled. Goodness, the way that girl carried on you'd think it had been the wedding of the queen of England."

She put a hand on her husband's shoulder, questioningly, and he cast her a swift smile.

"I'll be up shortly, dear."

Bernice had no questions for this; she nodded, gave him a tired smile, and pressed a kiss to her son's forehead as she left the kitchen. The two Connor men sat silent for a moment, turning their whiskey glasses around and around in front of them.

Finally, Martin heaved a sigh.

"Reckon I might as well get it over with. It's about Linda Mallory."

Val felt every muscle within him tense at the sound of her name. Though he had half expected it, his body's reaction still took him by surprise.

"I figured it might be," he managed to force out between tightly pressed lips. "You looked too serious for it to be much else. Either that or something to do with the ranch."

His father sighed.

"Well, there's a bit about that, too," he said. "The one sort of leads to the other."

"Tell me, Pa."

"It's been six months since the last letter, hasn't it? Six months since she bothered to write you and let you know whether she was alive or dead. That's not the way a bride should behave, now, is it. Not the way any respectable woman should treat the man who cares about her. And the way you've been moping around, Val – well, I couldn't bear it, to be honest."

Val tried to smile, but it felt more like a grimace.

"Aw, gee, I'm sorry, Pa," he said. "Reckon I should have kept my worryin' to myself a little better."

His father eyed him sharply.

"Is that sarcasm, Percival Connor?"

"No, sir. Well. Maybe a little."

"I won't listen to it, Val. You're not a boy, angry at your father. You're a grown man."

Val sighed and rubbed at his forehead.

"I know it. I'm sorry, Pa. I guess I just get – overwhelmed with it all, sometimes."

Martin nodded, looking slightly discomfited.

"I reckon you would," he said. "Reckon I would, too. Anyone would. And that's why I had to put an end to it."

Val turned a wide-eyed gaze on him, waiting for the explanation. His father closed his own eyes for a moment, and a look crossed over his face as though something had pained him. Then he took in a deep breath, and carried on.

"I went to Timothy Barrow and explained the situation to him. Oh, he knew part of it – but if you weren't so goldurned prideful, Val, and had told him a little more, he might have said more to you than he did. This isn't the first time that it's happened, it seems."

"What exactly has happened, Pa?"

He kept his tone as even and controlled as he could, though the words were fighting with him, anxious to get out and not caring at what level they emerged.

"This Miss Mallory – she's a heartbreaker, Val. You're not the first one. In her own town, she managed to set two young men against each other – brothers, in fact. They fought a duel, in the end, and though no lives were lost, the family never recovered from it. That was why her poor mother sent her off down here, to get her away from those two poor boys. But she set her cap for you, instead."

Val shook his head. His throat was dry, and swallowing was painful.

"She didn't," he croaked. "She never did – she hardly would look at me at first…"

"Oh, I wouldn't say that she wasn't artful in it," Martin said heavily. "She had us all fooled, didn't she? Even her uncle, who didn't know a thing about it until later. But she strung you along, led you by the nose, sure as shootin'. And when she went home, why, the first thing that little girl did was go to one of the brothers and tell them all about her new beau down in Culver's Creek and how he couldn't bear to live without her – well." He stopped, gathering his thoughts, and then carried on. "Her ma knew the best thing was for a flirt like that to be married off, somewhere she couldn't do anymore damage. She arranged for Miss Mallory to marry a gentleman out in California. I reckon that girl never really intended any harm; it was a little fun for her, that was all. Well, she's got her work cut out for her now, as a wife."

Val stared at his father, unsure of what to say.

"Married – already?"

His father sighed again, and Val realized suddenly that this was just as painful for his father as it was for him.

"Val, she's been married near a year already. Her ma planned it right after she returned home from Culver's Creek. It seemed the safest."

"Then…her letter…"

"A letter from a married woman," Martin confirmed, nodding. "A handwritten, postage-stamped lie."

Val felt something in his heart, the last portion of it that had remained open and soft, begin to develop a shell, begin to close, begin to solidify.

"A lie," he said softly, and he stood up to pace.

His father let him be, recognizing that silent movement was the only acceptable substitute now for violent anger. Val had thought that his heart was already broken beyond repair; he had thought that nothing could touch it. Now, though, he understood the truth. He had known nothing, until now. The girl he'd loved did not love him back. She never had. And no matter how long he waited, she would never return.

"That's all," said his father at last, gently. "I figured I couldn't keep it from you, though I'd do anything to stop the hurt. You know I would."

Yes, his father had been the messenger of this heartbreak, but Val wouldn't have thanked him for hiding the truth. With an immense effort, he returned to the table and sat down, resting his hands palms-down in front of him.

"What was the other part?"

"Hmm?"

"The other part. Regarding the ranch. You have something else to tell me."

"Oh, that. Right." Martin shifted uncomfortably in his chair, chin dipped low, eyeing his son. "I wanted you to know the truth, however painful it might be, because you can't wait for that girl any longer. She's not coming back."

"I know, Pa. I understand that."

"And – that means, Val, that it's time for you to move on."

Val stared again at his father as Martin elucidated.

"You can't let a girl like that ruin your life. She didn't even do it intentionally, it was nothing but a prank, an accident, a way for her to occupy her time. You've got to let go of her memory, Val – and find someone else to marry."

In Val's chest, his heart of stone grew colder.

"Someone else," he repeated. "Marry – someone else."

"Yes."

"No."

"What was that, son?"

Val leaned forward, fixing his eyes on his father's haggard face.

"I won't do it," he said. "I won't marry anyone but the woman I love."

Martin sat back in his chair, his face awash with amazement.

"Val, she's married to someone else. And she never loved you – not like a good man like you should be loved."

"I know it. And that's all. I've given love all the chances it deserves, Pa – I won't be taken in again."

A long sigh escaped his father, and he nodded.

"I understand," he said. "I understand, son. It's hard enough to lose someone who loved you in return, but even harder to find that they didn't care about you to begin with. But you needn't make it a love match – not at first, anyhow. Find a good girl to marry, and I reckon you'll find that love follows afterwards, whether you mean it to or not."

Val blanched, blinking at his father in confusion.

"What do you mean?"

"I mean that plenty of marriages start out as arrangements, nothing more. You might find, given time, that you fall in love with your wife no matter."

"I don't believe that."

"Your belief doesn't make it untrue, son," Martin told him gently. "Just ask your ma."

Val opened his mouth and closed it again without speaking. Martin smiled.

"I figured that would give you something to think about," he said. "I didn't just say it for no reason, either. Listen, son – I know you're feeling angry, and hurt, and bitter, and all of it rightly so. But I won't let you throw your life away for all that. You need to get married, start a family. Put your thoughts on someone else, and you'll forget all about the pain."

"I can't do that, Pa. I can't."

"You can and you will. Else I'll find someone else to pass this ranch down to."

Val stared at his father in disbelief.

"You wouldn't."

"I would. I need to know that the ranch is being cared for – that your ma will be cared for, after I'm gone."

"Oh, Pa, you don't need to talk like that…"

"What I need or don't need to do isn't up to you, Percival Connor. Fact is, I'm putting it in my will, first thing tomorrow. This ranch only gets handed down to you if you marry and have a child – I'm not about to let my legacy end with myself, let alone an angry boy who can't get past a cruel trick some girl played on him."

The words were harsh, the tone sharp – but Val saw his father's face soften as their eyes met.

"Now, I don't mean to add to your burden," Martin said gently. "But I mean what I say. A wife and a child, or one of your brothers-in-law will have control of the ranch. And then it won't be Connor Ranch anymore, will it? Neither of us want that."

For a long time, they sat silent, chewing over what had been said – and what was left unsaid. Finally, Val said, "Just where am I supposed to find a girl to marry, Pa? I'm nearly a decade older than any unmarried girl in Culver's Creek, now – they're such a rare commodity, every one of 'em is snapped up at eighteen."

"Why not follow in Mrs. Mallory's footsteps, and write to a matrimonial agency? You needn't find someone in Missouri, let alone Culver's Creek. Your grandma was from back east, in Boston. Maybe you'd be better suited for a girl from further away."

"Boston," Val murmured. It sounded as far away as the moon, but he couldn't help but think that his father might be right. It hadn't gone so well, thus far, trying to marry someone closer to home. And if love was not the object, but simply matrimony – well, what did it matter how much they had in common?

He didn't want to marry anyone other than Linda Mallory, who had burned him so badly that a scar was left in her wake. Love held nothing for him anymore – not promise, not hope, not happiness. But his father was right – she had no right to ruin his life, and she certainly had no right to keep him from inheriting the ranch.

If his father wanted him to marry and have children, then that was what he would do.

For his parents' sake, if not his own.

CHAPTER 3

On the tenth of December, Isabelle Dollenberg stepped out of the train on the little platform at Culver's Creek and took a deep breath of what smelled like Christmas.

For the first time in forever, her heart filled with hope.

Snow on the ground, snow blanketing the rooftops and the pine trees, light feathery flakes falling all around her – she hadn't seen pristine snow like this since she was a little girl, visiting her grandmother in upstate Massachusetts. In Boston, the snow was muddied and dirtied with footprints, horse hooves, and wagon wheels almost as soon as it fell. Yes, it was glorious, almost magical…

And she decided to let it be a sign.

A sign that her match through Verseeve's Matrimonial Agency in Boston was going to be blessed.

Her breath hitched a little in her chest at the thought, squeezing tight, and she put a hand to her throat, trying to breathe deeply and calm herself. After all this time, after all the pain and the heartache, it seemed almost impossible to believe that this new life would be content, let alone happy. But Isabelle had always been the sort of girl to look on the bright side, and the past few years of tragedy had not been enough to change that fundamental trait. Yes, whatever came next, she was determined to throw her whole heart and soul into it.

Even if no one appeared to be there to greet her.

Clutching the large, worn carpetbag that held all her remaining worldly goods, she stepped forward and craned her neck, looking up and down the street. The terse description of Mr. Percival Connor provided by the matrimonial agency told her only that he was tall and dark haired, in his mid-twenties. There were few passersby on the street beyond the platform, and none of them seemed to match what she was looking for. A middle-aged man with a kindly face glanced at her, then stopped and gave her a longer, more searching look. Isabelle's heart skipped a beat or two, but she checked her instinct to turn away from him. This wasn't like it had been back home in Boston; this was a small town, and she was a stranger here. It only made sense that she would attract the attention of the locals. Besides, she needed help, and the genial friendliness of his face suggested that he wouldn't be averse to lending a hand if he could.

"Well, now, miss." he said. "You're a new face around these parts. Just step off the train, did you?"

She gulped and nodded.

"Yes – I've just arrived, and I'm not sure where to go next."

"No one there to collect you, eh? Well, where was it you were wanting to go?"

She took the letter of introduction from the agency from her pocket and handed it to him. He unfolded it and ran a slow and unpracticed eye over the words, then glanced up at her. There was a slightly bemused look on his face, and an undeniable twinkle of amusement in his eyes.

"Well, now. You're here for Mr. Connor, are you?"

She nodded.

"Yes – but perhaps he didn't receive the telegram from the agency and didn't know for certain when I would be coming."

"Could be, could be," the friendly stranger said, rubbing his chin. Yes, there was certainly a measure of amusement in his eyes. "I reckon that's it, miss. It hasn't got a thing to do with Val thinking twice and changing his mind – or letting his pride get the better of him. No, sir. I mean, ma'am."

Isabelle knew that the expression on her face must convey her confusion; she could feel it. The sort of expression that had always caused her mother to sigh in despair and beg her to look a little less gullible – the sort of expression that had always made Thomas grin and pull her hair teasingly. *Going too fast for you, am I, Bella?*

She shook the memory away from her, trying not to feel the ache in her heart. This was a new life. Her old life had no place here.

"If you please, sir," she said, determined not to let her confusion stop her from getting answers, "could you tell me how to get to Mr. Connor's house?"

"Well, now, miss, Connor Ranch is about a ten-minute walk to the south." He pointed to the left, down the street leading away from the larger buildings that surrounded them. "It's awful cold out there today, though. And a girl as pretty as you shouldn't be slogging through the snow. Maybe you'd better come home with me, and I'll saddle up the horse and take you out there."

He was right; it was very cold. But the last thing she wanted was to show up on the doorstep of her husband to be, with this fellow acting as her savior. Kindly he undoubtedly was, but there was a familiar gleam in his eyes when he looked at her, a gleam that she had spent years walking away from on the streets of Boston.

"Thank you, sir, but I'm quite used to the cold, and I can manage. Ten minutes to the south, you say?"

He nodded, pushing his hat back on his head.

"That's so. Well, you keep my offer in mind, little lady, and if you get to Connor Ranch and they don't treat you right, you come right back into town and ask around for Teller Smith. I'd be pleased as punch to make sure you were taken care of."

The longer she spoke to him, the more the gleam in his eyes seemed to grow. She nodded her thanks, managed a polite smile, and turned to go. It wasn't until she was several blocks away from him that her hands relaxed enough to allow her knuckles, with her hand clutched tightly around the handle of the bag, to fade from dead white.

Perhaps that was what she missed the most, about Thomas – feeling as though she belonged to someone, and no one else could touch her. Mr. Smith had been very friendly, and she knew enough to suppose that she had been in no danger, in the middle of the street, in the middle of the day. She was overreacting. But she never had gotten used to fellows paying her such dedicated attention, and it still made her nervous. When she was married again, she wouldn't have to worry about such things. She would only be thinking of her husband...

And if this Mr. Percival Connor happened to look at her with that gleam in his eye, perhaps she wouldn't mind in the least.

She did hope, though, that they would have a little time to get to know each other before they got married. It was one thing to pick up and travel so many hundreds of miles away, choosing to start her life over again. It was another to arrive in Culver's Creek, Missouri one day and find herself married that very afternoon.

Yes, a little time wouldn't be amiss – but not too much. She was anxious to get her new life started, and the wedding was the most important step.

Her daydreaming about the life ahead kept her occupied as she walked along the road. The snow was only about four inches deep, just enough to soften the edges of the world. The thin, wispy clouds that had covered the sun drifted off as though distracted, letting the sunlight spark brilliance everywhere around her. It was beautiful enough to keep her from thinking too much about the cold.

Before too long, she saw a snow-covered sign ahead.

Connor, was all it said.

Her heart picked up, thumping faster. She was getting close – closer than ever to meeting the man who would be her husband. She turned off the road, following the sign, and found herself on a deeply-rutted pathway that showed signs of horse hooves, tramping back and forth and mussing up the smoothness of the snow. The road bent around a stand of fir trees, and just around the curve the ranch house came into view. It was a large, sprawling building, neat and well-kept, with two outbuildings behind it. One appeared to have suffered the impact of a downed tree, and was half-crushed on one side. The remains of the culprit were still in evidence, though she could see three figures working alongside it, and heard the rasping sound of a two-man saw, signifying that the destruction would, at least, not be completely pointless.

Ahead of her, the ranch house waited. A neatly swept flagstone pathway led up to the veranda, which was also cleared of snow. The Connors took good care of their property, that much was evident.

Swallowing hard past the lump in her throat, she ascended the stairs and knocked timidly on the front door.

A moment of silence passed, and then she heard a voice, getting louder as the speaker came closer.

"I don't know what you're playin' at, Agnes, but if we don't get that pie in the oven soon it'll never be ready in time for supper, and you know how Mr. Connor likes his apple pie with his coffee. Land sakes, girl, anybody would think you'd just set foot in a kitchen this morning, instead of working here for three years, and now there's someone at the door, and I haven't even had a moment to myself all…"

The door was pulled open, revealing a woman in her later years. It was only her iron-gray hair that marked her age so strongly; otherwise, her features were quite youthful, and despite the mild irritation in her voice, she immediately gave Isabelle a welcoming, if bemused, smile.

"Hello, miss – can I help you?"

Isabelle held her bag in front of her, holding onto it tightly with both hands.

"Excuse me, ma'am, this is the Connor residence, isn't it?"

"Yes, dear, it certainly is."

"And – Mr. Connor lives here...Mr. Percival Connor, that is?"

The woman narrowed her eyes at her, as though speculating as to Isabelle's intentions, and then suddenly a light came over her pretty face. Her eyes widened, her eyebrows raised, and she reached out to Isabelle with both hands.

"Goodness, you must be the bride. The girl, I mean – the girl the matrimonial agency sent. Goodness gracious, come on in, my dear. Your hands are freezing. Did you walk all this way? You can't have done. Oh, if only I had known you were coming today, I would have collected you myself. Agnes. Run and fetch Val from the barn, would you?"

"Right away, Mrs. Connor." The second voice came from down the hall, and there was a clatter and then the slam of a door. Evidently Agnes took her mission very seriously.

Isabelle gaped at the older woman.

"Mrs. Connor? You must be Mr. Percival Connor's mother, then?"

Mrs. Connor twinkled at her.

"I am – but you must call me Bernice. And your name is Isabelle, isn't it?"

Isabelle nodded. "Yes. Isabelle Dollenberg."

"That's right. I saw the letter from the agency. Such a pretty name, Isabelle. Oh, my dear, you won't believe how delighted we all are to have you here. Come on into the kitchen, and I'll fix you a cup of tea. We'll warm you up right away."

Isabelle followed her in gratefully, glad to feel the warmth from the cheerful kitchen fire. The house was cozily appointed, and there appeared to be a doily on every available surface. Warm, clean, and a little jumbled – it was a home full of love, she was certain of that even before she met the rest of the family. It made a part of her heart ache, the part that still thought of Thomas and the baby every day, no matter how hard she tried to bury the memories.

"Sit down, my dear, and warm your hands with this mug. There's milk in the jug, sugar in the pot – we drink tea at a moment's notice in this house, and there's always more where that came from. Especially in the winter. Goodness, you poor thing, having to travel through this weather. Was the train terribly cold?"

"Not terribly," Isabelle said, smiling. "A little. But I had a scarf and a blanket with me, along with my coat, and I was all right, I think. No harm done, and I'm glad to be here at last."

Bernice Connor opened her mouth to reply – another something sympathetic, Isabelle thought, by the expression on the older woman's face – but the door to the kitchen was flung open, and an older man strode in. He was tall, broad-shouldered, and in his weather-beaten face, blue eyes twinkled with energy and life. He swept his hat off, revealing a head full of gray hair.

"Well, well. This must be the famous Miss Dollenberg."

"Martin. You've scattered snow all over my clean floor." his wife scolded him, taking him by the arm and directing him toward the fire. He smiled down at her and chucked her under the chin apologetically; there was obvious affection between them, and it made Isabelle smile even as she felt a faint blush coming over her cheeks.

"Well, Agnes will just have to sweep it up again, won't she, Agnes?"

The maid, following closely along behind them, laughed as she bent obediently with a broom and dustpan.

"Poor Agnes," said Bernice Connor, shaking her head.

Her husband sat down next to Isabelle and held a hand toward her.

"Martin Connor," he said. "Val's father. He'll be along in a few minutes – he had something to finish up, I suppose."

"That boy," said Bernice. Evidently shaking her head at the men in her family was a regular occurrence. "Only he would insist on finishing some chore when the woman he's going to marry has come all the way from Boston and just now arrived. And in the snow, no less."

"It's not snowing too hard, at least," Martin Connor said. "He'll be ready for a sit-down by the fire, I reckon, all the same." He turned his attention back to Isabelle. "Well, now, Miss Dollenberg. You're very welcome to our little ranch."

She smiled back at him. He was a warm, lively man, that much was clear – though there was an undertone to his voice, something in his eyes, that she didn't quite understand. A sort of sadness, not quite onstage but waiting in the wings...

"Thank you very much, Mr. Connor. I'm pleased to be here, as I was just telling your wife. And, of course, I understand that you and your son must be very busy. Er – when you say 'Val,' you do mean...your son Percival, don't you?"

Mr. Connor laughed.

"I do, indeed," he said. "Martin Percival Connor – named for his father in the first instance and for his grandfather in the second. Well, we couldn't very well have two Martins running around the place, and I wasn't about to insist that the poor boy be called Percival. We tried all sorts of things, didn't we, wife? Percy...Perry..."

"M.P.," put in Bernice, smiling over her shoulder.

"But in the end, Val is what stuck. And it's a good name for my son, Miss Dollenberg, for he's valiant indeed."

"I'm sure he is."

"He's a hard worker, too, as you might expect from the fact that he's still out there in the snow. And he's kind hearted. Takes after his mother in that respect." He shot his wife a mischievous glance, which she returned swiftly. "In short, Miss Dollenberg, it's not just a father's natural pride that leads me to say that my son is one of the finest men in Culver's Creek, if not the whole of Missouri. I reckon you two will be very happy together."

It was a hope so earnestly stated that it caught at Isabelle's heart. What a wonderful thing, for Percival Connor to have a father who so clearly wanted nothing more than his son's happiness. She could only hope that he would get his wish – though she could not help but feel the remnants of her long-held doubt.

"Mr. Connor, while we're on the subject of names…"

"Please, call me Martin, my dear."

"Martin – thank you. And if you don't mind – please call me Isabelle. It's easier than – than my full name." She lowered her eyes to the table, feeling her heartbeat quicken a little. "You see, it isn't Miss Dollenberg, really."

Martin Connor raised his eyebrows.

"No? The message from the agency must have been wrong."

"No, it isn't that. Dollenberg is my name – my married name. Mrs. Isabelle Dollenberg, you see."

The kitchen was quiet for a moment, and she glanced up just in time to see Martin and Bernice Connor exchange surprised glances.

"My husband was Thomas Dollenberg," Isabelle explained quietly. "I'm a widow – oh, for almost a year now."

Martin Connor's eyes fixed on hers again, and this time they were filled with sympathy.

"You poor girl," he said. "A widow, and so young."

"I'm sorry about the misunderstanding. I did tell the agency, I promise I wasn't trying to keep anything a secret."

"No, of course not, my dear." He reached over and patted her hand, a bit clumsily but with kindness. "I reckon they played mum for reasons of their own." He eyed her for a moment. "You – you got on well with your husband?"

Isabelle bit her lip and nodded, hoping that she could keep her emotions at bay.

"I did," she said. "Very well. I loved him very much, though we were not married long. But I promise you, Mr. Connor – I made the decision to marry again of my own free will, and I was not coerced by anyone or anything. I can't guarantee that your son and I will have a marriage of true love, but I can promise that I will do my earthly best to be a good wife to him – the best wife I can be."

He gazed into her eyes for a long moment and then nodded.

"Well, my dear," he said, his joviality momentarily quieted. "I don't reckon anyone could ask any more of you than that." He glanced to the floor as though suddenly distracted. "Shall we fetch your bags from the train before the snow begins to pile up?"

"Oh, I haven't any other bags. Just my old carpetbag."

"Is that all?" He raised an eyebrow. "I reckon most women would show up with at least two trunks in tow."

"I sold most of my things before I left," she said, straining to keep her voice even. She wouldn't think about them – she wouldn't think about what she had sold, or the things she had given away. There was so much that she could scarcely bear to part with, and yet they were all remnants of the life she had left behind, the life she led before coming to Culver's Creek. It hadn't seemed right to pack her life up and drag it with her.

"Well, we'll be right glad to take you into the mercantile and order you whatever you need," put in Bernice, giving her a warm smile. "George stocks all sorts of things, and what he doesn't have, he can order for you."

Isabelle smiled back, her heart warming. "Thank you. I don't need much. I'm used to a very simple life."

"That's good, good," said Martin, nodding with satisfaction. "A simple life is what we all need, eh, Bernice? Especially after three weddings in two years…"

Bernice chuckled.

"That's so, Martin – I reckon we've had all the excitement we're due for some time."

It was on the tip of Isabelle's tongue to ask about this – who got married, and how was it that they were married three times? It made no sense to her – but the kitchen door was pushed open once more and another man stepped in. A younger man – broad-shouldered, with a thick thatch of black hair that was slightly longer than the current fashion and covered in snowflakes. His features were regular and pleasing, but it was his eyes that caught her attention at once – dark eyes, with a depth and a strength to them that seemed to call to something similar inside herself, somewhere deeply buried. Something she hadn't even known she had…

Her mouth had gone dry, she realized suddenly, and her eyes were fixed on his in a frank stare. She tore her gaze away at once, but not before a blush came over her cheeks.

"There you are, Val," said Bernice, pushing her much larger son toward the table. "Now, go and warm up, and don't say that you've got to go back out there into the barn to finish some chore…"

"But I do, Ma."

"…because your father's the one who runs the ranch, and he'll excuse you for the evening, won't he, Martin?"

Martin grinned at his son.

"Don't reckon I've got much choice."

"Percival Connor, sit down and introduce yourself politely to Miss – sorry, dear, Mrs. Dollenberg."

Steeling herself, Isabelle turned her eyes back to the man she was going to marry. She feared she would see a look of surprise – or, worse, of distaste – but she saw no such expression on the handsome face of the man who stood over her, only a vague curiosity. He held a hand out to her and she took it.

"Sorry my fingers are cold," he said. "I reckon Pa told you I was out finishing things up for the afternoon. I guess I lost track of time. I ought to have been there to greet you at the station."

She swallowed hard.

"No matter," she managed. "I found my way here with the help of a friendly fellow in town who was so kind as to point me in the right direction."

"Friendly fellow, eh?" His eyebrows raised. "Who might that be, or didn't you get his name?"

"Er – yes, I think it was Mr. Smith."

"Teller Smith," put in Martin Connor, chuckling into his mug of coffee. "Hah."

Isabelle glanced from him back to his son, knowing that her expression betrayed her confusion.

Percival Connor gave a wry smile.

"Teller Smith's always got an eye on the main chance," he said. "A pretty girl like you walks into town, and he's bound to know it the minute you set foot off the train. Oh, well. You made it here safely, and I reckon that's all that matters."

Isabelle was caught between blushing at her own confusion and blushing in pleasure at the fact that he had called her pretty – either way, the result appeared to be a blush, no matter how hard she fought against it.

"Val, why don't you show poor Isabelle where her room is? I'm sure she'd like the chance to freshen up and rest a little before supper."

"Sure, Ma." He nodded at Isabelle and bent to pick up her bag, lifting the heavy piece of baggage as though it were lighter than a feather, as though it contained nothing but air. Isabelle was starting to feel similarly light-headed. She got up from the table and followed him through the hallway to the stairs. He led the way up and to a room at the end of the upstairs hallway, the door of which stood open.

"Here you are, Mrs. Dollenberg."

To hear his easy, unquestioning use of her married name, her heart fluttered strangely. Wasn't he at least curious? Didn't he want to know anything about her past? Well, perhaps this just wasn't the time for it. After all, she was very tired, and no doubt it was obvious to all three of the Connors. She slipped past him into the room. The bed, with the covers turned down and the curtains around the window drawn against the weak light of the winter afternoon, looked very inviting.

Percival Connor set her bag down in the corner of the room and turned to face her.

"Well," he said.

"Well," she echoed him faintly. "I – I hear that you are called Val."

He nodded. "Yes – you can call me that, too, if you want."

"Val – please, call me Isabelle. We might as well get started on getting to know each other, don't you think? As we're going to be married...very soon."

The last few words were difficult to speak. After all, they hadn't discussed how soon the wedding would take place at all. And the mention his parents had made about three weddings happening recently – she was doubly curious, no, triply so. Might Val Connor not have his own history? But it was silly to think that the marriages were his, of course – still, a man as handsome as him couldn't have gone unnoticed by all the young women in the vicinity.

He regarded her quietly for a moment, seeming to be trying to sum her up in his own head.

Then he said, "I reckon we'll take just as long as we need. No rush."

She couldn't help but feel somewhat deflated. "Oh."

But then he flashed a grin, almost – it seemed – despite himself.

"Anyhow, the preacher's been run just about ragged marrying my three little sisters off. He needs a break. At least for a few days."

The smile, and the joking, teasing tone, brought warmth back into Isabelle. She smiled back and, seizing the impulse, reached out and laid a hand on his arm.

"I know we don't know much about each other, Val Connor," she said. "But I promised your father already, and I'll promise you the same – I intend to be the best wife I can be to you, and do everything I can to make our future a happy one."

If she had hoped for some grand revelation of feeling, some show of the connection between them, she was disappointed. Val Connor looked at her for a moment longer, and then gave a single swift nod.

"Get some rest, Isabelle," he said. "We've got plenty of time to talk things over later on."

And then he was gone, leaving her alone in her new room, wondering whether she had imagined the brief flash of fire in his eyes – and what it meant.

CHAPTER 4

I'll promise you – I intend to be the best wife I can be to you and do everything I can to make our future a happy one.

Val leaned his head against the warm flank of the cow. Nearly a foot of snow had fallen over the past night, and he was grateful for the warmth of the barn, blanketed and protected by the frozen buildup and kept warm with the heat of the ranch's ten dairy cows. The last of the milk hissed into the bucket, and he stood up reluctantly, patting the cow on the side.

"Good girl, Bess," he murmured. "You show 'em how it's done, eh? The best cream in Culver's Creek comes from Connor Ranch, and it's because we've got the best cows."

He gave her a final affectionate slap and moved away from the stalls, whistling to the others. He couldn't help feeling a certain pride of ownership, even though the ranch wasn't his – yet. It would be someday. If all went well...

I intend to be the best wife I can be to you...

Besides, it only made sense that he would feel proud of the ranch. After all, he'd grown up here. It was all tied in to the pride and joy of the family name. It reflected the honorable reputation his father had built up, and the love between Martin and Bernice, and even the joyful marriages of the three Connor girls...

It represented everyone, it seemed, except for Val, who had been left out in the cold...

I'll promise you –

...until now.

Try though he might, he could not get Isabelle's words out of his head. It had both startled and enchanted him to hear her speak so freely, and make such a big promise, without the slightest provocation. Without hardly knowing him, even. They were going to be married, certainly, but to promise him every effort at happiness – well, he wasn't sure how to feel about it. Happiness, married to a woman he didn't know? A woman who wasn't Linda Mallory? A woman he had only agreed to marry because his father insisted that he pass on the family name, or he wouldn't inherit the ranch he loved so dearly?

To promise marriage was one thing. To promise happiness was quite another.

That was how he felt about it, deep down – resentful. As though Isabelle Dollenberg was promising him something she had no right to.

And yet…

And yet, he couldn't help but admit to himself that the idea wasn't entirely unlikely. There was a warmth and kindness in her eyes that he liked, and there was no denying that she was very, very pretty.

I'll do everything I can to make our future a happy one.

The confusion in his own head was nothing short of frustrating, and he resolved once again to push the thought of Isabelle Dollenberg and her luminous eyes to the back of his mind. This was easier said than done, he found, as he entered the ranch house and was greeted by his father.

"That's it for today."

Val blinked at him.

"What do you mean by that, Pa?"

"I mean exactly what I say. That's it today – you're to stay indoors and talk with Isabelle."

Val frowned.

"Pa, you know as well as I do that there's plenty more to be done today. We can't afford to take a day off from work just because we have a visitor. Besides, Ma can keep her occupied – Agnes doesn't come in today, and I'm sure Mrs. Dollenberg will be happy to help."

"I'm sure she would, too – she looks like a girl who knows the meaning of hard work, and no one's more appreciative of that than me, after raising three of my own. But that's all besides the point."

"But Pa…"

"I didn't say I was taking the day off," Martin said, overriding him. "I only said that you are to do so. In fact, you'd better take the rest of the week."

"Pa."

The idea of work mounting up, never to be caught up to again, swam dizzily through Val's brain, but his father would brook no argument.

"You've got something important to see to – something more important than chores on the ranch. Anyone can do those. Isabelle needs your attention, Val – your attention, and your interest, and your efforts, do you hear me? If the two of you are to be married, you'll need a chance to get to know each other first."

Val shook his head, feeling suddenly helpless in the face of his father's determination.

"Why now, Pa?" he said quietly. "Why did you have to insist that I get married now?"

After a long moment, Martin's face softened.

"Miss Mallory moved on with her life," he said. "Some time ago. It's well overdue that you did as well. You may think that you need time to mourn her – but the truth is, she's not dead. She just never loved you, Val, like you should be loved. There's nothing worth mourning in that."

He put a hand on Val's shoulder, ignoring his son's flinch.

"Spend some time with Isabelle. She's a sweet girl."

"You don't even know her, Pa."

"I know sweetness when I see it, and that girl's got it in spades. Give her a chance."

Val clenched his jaw.

"I'm only marrying her because you want me to, Pa," he reminded his father. "Because you insist that I have a child to pass down the family name. Asking me to be happy about it is – well, it's asking a little much. I'll never love anyone like I loved Linda Mallory."

In the rueful smile that crossed his father's face, Val recognized himself.

"I hope not," Martin said. "You'd better love her far more deeply, truly, and lastingly than that – that disloyal female."

He grinned. "Never say never, son. At least you've got to give it a try."

Val sighed. Above him, he could hear footsteps as the rest of the house began to stir.

"I make no promises," he said. "But I'll try."

"Good man."

As his father rose and went to greet his mother, Val watched them, fighting the urge to shake his head. Why couldn't his father understand? It was clear that Martin and Bernice still shared a love that was evergreen, even after four children and all these years. Why couldn't he see that that was what Val wanted for himself?

Why was he so insistent that his only son settle for something less?

CHAPTER 5

"Well, now." Martin said jovially, rubbing his hands together. "What do you think?"

"I think it's a dirt trap," said his wife crisply. "And – Martin. There are pine needles all over my clean floor."

"Agnes will just have to clean them up – won't you, Agnes?" He looked around himself. "Agnes?"

"Agnes is gone until after the first of the year," Bernice told him. "You said she ought to – don't you remember?"

Val caught the look of vague confusion on his father's face and knew that Martin had no memory of doing such a thing. But it didn't matter; Agnes had been delighted to be given three weeks off, and she wasn't about to come back to the

Connor home just to sweep up after the installation of the Christmas tree.

"Anyhow, they're fir needles, not pine," Martin said, throwing an arm around his wife and hugging her tightly. "What do you think about it, Isabelle? Your first Missouri Christmas tree."

Isabelle smiled at him, and it warmed Val's heart as it always seemed to do. In the four days since she had arrived in Culver's Creek, she had quickly found her way into the hearts of the Connor family – at least, the hearts of Martin and Bernice. Val still felt compelled to reserve judgement. But there was no denying that her smile was very warm and very genuine and – very pretty…

"I think it's beautiful. Well worth a little sweeping up, and I'm happy to do it."

"Thank you, dear," Martin told her. "You see, Bernice? If Isabelle likes it, it's worth all the huffing and puffing to get it into the sitting room. Let alone the needles."

"Huffing and puffing and blowing the house down," said Bernice, chuckling. "It's the biggest tree we've ever had," she explained to Isabelle. "I suppose we've got you to thank for it. Someone's set out to be impressive."

But Martin was unmoved by her teasing. Eyes fixed on the tree, he gazed rapturously up at it. Val thought that he had never seen his father look quite so proud.

"You never know which tree will be the last," Martin said. "Might as well make every Christmas as good as can be, eh?" He glanced over at Val, and Val was startled to see a paleness in his father's face, and a glimmer in his eye. Was he not feeling well? He was on the verge of asking, but Martin turned away again and clapped his hands together. "Now all it needs is to be decorated. Tinsel, candy canes, and a star atop the highest branch – Val, I leave it in your capable hands. I reckon Isabelle will be ready and willing to help you."

Val glanced at Isabelle, just in time to catch her eyes fall on his, swiftly.

"Oh, I don't know," she started.

"Nonsense."

"But – I'm not very good at decorating the tree…"

"Val will be there. Between the two of you, you'll sort everything out. I have every confidence." He put his arm around Bernice's shoulders again and turned her toward the door. "As for you, my dear, I don't suppose you could make me some coffee…"

They walked out together, Bernice still under her husband's arm. Val gave Isabelle a helpless grin.

"I guess she forgot about being irritated over the pine needles," Isabelle said softly.

"I guess she did. Listen, Isabelle, it's just that Pa is determined that we should spend time together, that's all. You likely noticed that he's been trying to arrange things all this past week…"

She smiled suddenly, as though she couldn't quite help herself.

"Yes, I didn't miss that," she said. "He's very – determined, your father, isn't he?"

"That's one word for it."

"I couldn't help but notice that he set us next to each other at the table."

"He did."

"And he seems to have given you some time away from your work…"

Val clenched his jaw a little, then forced himself to relax it again. It wasn't her fault that she didn't realize how much he chafed against being ordered to keep away from his duties on the ranch…or how worried he was over what might be happening while he wasn't there.

"He has," he said. "Chores, he calls them. I reckon he figures anyone can do them, and it needn't be me."

Isabelle gave him a soft, hesitant smile.

"I know they're more than just chores," she said. "And if I do, I'm sure your father does, too."

Her warm reassurance, however timidly spoken, touched his heart – and he tried to push it away, as he pushed away everything that hinted at a deeper connection between the two of them.

"All I'm trying to say," he said, gruffly, "is that you needn't help with the tree if you don't want to. It's only Pa's way."

"Oh. I see – yes, I understand. But I'll help you, Val, if you'd like me too. I only..." Her voice quavered a little. "Will you do the higher branches, please, and let me do the lower ones? I'm not fond of heights."

It was the first hint of her having any sort of fear at all, and he gave her a quizzical glance as he opened up the box of tinsel and well-wrapped glass ornaments.

"Heights, eh? The top of the tree can't be more than six feet. I can reach it standing."

"Then do so, if you don't mind. Thank you."

He hesitated for a moment, reluctant to ask but driven by curiosity. What was the source of her strange fear? He held back, knowing that hearing the truth might build his sympathy for her – and might cause her pain.

Finally, as they worked together in silence, he couldn't help himself.

"If you want to talk about it…"

It was nothing but an offer, thrown out there to be taken advantage of or left entirely, he told himself. The sort of offer any gentleman should make to a woman in obvious distress, regardless of whether the two of them are due to be married. His father thought that he needed to get to know Isabelle Dollenberg – well, this appeared to be a prime opportunity.

"About what?" she said softly.

Now he felt stupid.

"About – why you're afraid of heights."

She was quiet for long enough that he thought she wasn't going to answer him at all, and had railed against himself for even trying. But then she turned to him, and his heart clenched within him to see tears shining in her eyes.

"Last Christmas," she said, and took a deep breath. "I had a – a fall."

He knew better than to speak and prompt her, this time around, letting her choose her own time to continue.

"I was putting the star on the top of the tree – the chair I was standing on was not strong enough to hold me. One of the legs came loose, and when I stepped on top of it, it buckled. I was reaching up, with my hands above my head." She stopped speaking and turned her head away. "I had nothing soft to break my fall, and no one was at home with me. I'd been decorating the tree to surprise Thomas – to surprise my husband."

The thought of the chair not being strong enough to hold such a small and delicate woman seemed next to impossible, but Val knew better than to question it. It was obvious that the memory still carried a great deal of pain along with it, and he got down on his knees beside her without even thinking about it, putting a hand on her arm.

"I'm sorry," he said. "You must have been hurt badly."

She bit her lip.

"Yes – badly."

"That's why you're afraid of heights."

"Yes." She looked up at the tree. The flickering firelight glimmered in her eyes.

"Thomas found you, though?" he prompted her gently. He couldn't help the flicker of curiosity that stirred within him at the mention of her first husband. From the moment he had realized that she was a widow, he had pushed away all questions regarding her past, unwilling to think of her as anything other than his parentally mandated bride in a marriage strictly of convenience. But this little detail about the Christmas tree opened a door that he had tried to keep closed. The woman beside him was just that: a woman. And he couldn't help but wonder what it was that had led her here.

"Eventually," she said. "I laid there for – oh, I don't know how long. He had been away – he drove a delivery wagon and carried to three other towns outside of Boston. But he came home, and he stayed there and nursed me back to health for two weeks, until the day after Christmas."

"He must have been a good man."

She nodded, and the tears in her eyes swelled larger, more present, as though they were about to spill over at any moment.

"He was a very good man," she said. "He threw himself back into his work as soon as he was able, as soon as I – as soon as he knew that I was going to be all right. Just one day we had. Just one day after Christmas."

Val had a sinking feeling that he knew what was going to come next.

Isabelle lowered her head, and he saw the tears spill over at last.

"It was an accident," she said. "The delivery wagon stuck in the mud, and when he tried to pull it free, it overturned onto him. The horse ran and dragged it. They said that he died very suddenly, and there was no pain. And I believe them, Val, I do – for I felt it all, his pain and mine. It came onto me that same day, and I've been running away from it ever since." She took a deep, shaky breath. "I'm sorry to be telling you all of this – we scarcely know each other."

Val shook his head.

"Don't be sorry," he said gently. "We know each other better, now."

Feeling as though he was watching from somewhere outside himself, he drew her gently into his arms. She came to him willingly, burying her head on his shoulder and stifling her sobs against his shirt. He held onto her delicate frame tightly, as though she was something precious. She knew the same thing that he did, and he understood it now. They both knew what it meant to lose the one you love the most.

CHAPTER 6

In the end, Val Connor didn't return to the fields to work on his beloved ranch until the day before Christmas. Isabelle Dollenberg wasn't sure how she felt about that.

On one hand, it was flattering. Flattering to know that he had agree to take a whole week away from his work, however grudgingly, just to get to know her. Even more flattering that he did not return as soon as his father allowed him to, simply because they were enjoying their time together. Oh, he helped around the house, always willing to lend a hand whenever needed by his mother or Isabelle herself. But his eyes strayed again and again to the window, as the snows mounted one day and melted the next, and she knew that his heart was outside in the acreage.

And so she regretted his decision to stay inside with her, no matter how deeply it flattered her.

She had promised him that she would do everything she could to make him happy – she'd promised his parents, too. How could she keep him away from the ranch and still count herself as faithful to that promise?

Still, it took all the self control she had to talk him into going back out on the morning of Christmas Eve.

"Are you sure that's what you want? After all, there's a lot of cooking and cleaning that goes into making Christmas supper. You might need my help."

She laughed, shaking her head.

"You heard your ma say that all three of your sisters will be here to help – not to mention their husbands. I think we can all get along without you for a day or two. More than the ranch can. It needs you."

"You've only been here a week and a half," he told her, grinning teasingly. "I don't know if I can honestly say that we've gotten to know each other well in just a week and a half. I reckon we need a little more time."

"Goodness, Percival Connor, leave the girl alone, she's got things to do," Bernice said as she entered the kitchen. "The two of you have all the time in the world to get to know each other better – either before your wedding, or after it."

Val's eyes caught Isabelle's and held them for a moment before he winked.

"Reckon it'll be easier after," he said. "All right, Ma, I'm going out to join Pa in the northern pasture. I hope the hands got that fence back up last week, but I haven't had a chance to look. I'll see you later."

"Goodbye, Val – until later."

He went out the kitchen door, and Isabelle went to the window, watching his tall, strong figure move through the snow drifts. Without realizing it, she gave a faint sigh, and was startled to hear Bernice laugh.

"What is it?"

"You, my dear." Bernice twinkled at her. "You really like our Val, don't you? Oh, you needn't even answer that – I can tell by the blush."

Blush or not, Isabelle felt that she ought to answer regardless.

"I do," she said simply. "I do like him. I suppose I ought to, as we're going to get married. And, after all, we have spent the last several days getting to know each other."

Bernice regarded her for a moment with a kindly smile.

"You have, at that. I know what happened to your husband, my dear – he mentioned it to his father and me. He was deeply touched by your devotion to him, and how much love you had for him, even now."

Isabelle felt a lump appear in her throat, and she swallowed past it as best as she could.

"Yes," she said. "I still love Thomas – but that won't stop me from loving Val, too."

"I know, dear. You and I both understand that a person can love more than once – and that each love is its own special sort. My own self, when I was young, I was certain I was going to marry a fellow named McCardy – James McCardy, he was, and he was from the same little town I grew up in. Oh, but I loved that boy."

Isabelle raised her eyebrows, hoping that her shock at this revelation was not as overwhelming as it felt.

"But you and Martin – you seem so ideally suited."

Bernice chuckled.

"That comes with time, my dear. Time, and growing up together. James and I only had a very brief courtship before I knew that he wouldn't make the sort of husband I wanted. He was a charmer, but a schemer, too, and I needed someone steady, someone I could trust. We all need that, dear. Oh, I still think of James with fondness – but when I moved out to live with my maiden aunt and met Martin, I knew then what true love really felt like, what it really meant. I knew what a good man could really be." She smiled, shaking her head.

"But some folks need more convincing than I did. My son is one of 'em."

Isabelle turned her eyes back to the window, feeling her heart sink a little.

"Is he?" she said. "I thought he might be – I thought, how could a man like Val Connor go unnoticed by the women around him?"

"Well, there have been precious few of them, for one thing. Culver's Creek isn't exactly teeming with sweet young maidens."

"Is that why he wrote for a mail order bride?"

"In the end – yes."

Isabelle swallowed. That pain in her throat wasn't lessening; if anything, it hurt even more.

"But before that," she prompted softly.

"Before that – Val was in love with a girl who treated him badly. My son can be prideful and rash, he can be stubborn and selfish, but he's a good man, and he fights against those sins with his whole being. And he was treated far worse than he could ever deserve, for his sins."

"What did she do?" Isabelle whispered.

"She didn't love him." Bernice's tone, so loving and warm when speaking about her son, turned bitter and cold as a stone thrown through a window. "She loved his adoration, but she didn't love him. Oh, she had more selfish pride than anyone, and she was young. Too young to know how much it hurt, to be led on as he was. But that's no excuse." She sighed. "Val had made up his mind that he would never marry."

"What changed his mind?"

"Oh, I suppose you could say his father helped him to see the light." She put a comforting arm around Isabelle's shoulders, joining her at the window. "Everyone needs to be shown a little light, now and then. And it's Christmas – what better time for it, eh?"

As she went about her chores around the house, helping in the kitchen and keeping the fire going in the sitting room for later, Isabelle found her thoughts returning again and again to the story she had just been told. Poor Val. The pain he must have felt – the pain of loss, and even worse, the pain of rejection. It put his behavior, his lack of curiosity and interest in her, in an entirely different light. She couldn't say but that she might herself feel just as he did, were she in his situation.

A heart could be broken in a hundred different ways...

But through her pondering, she found reason for hope. Val had evidently made up his mind not to love again, but she truly believed that he was warming up to her already. And certainly Bernice and Martin seemed to think so. It was nothing solid, but it was certainly reason for cheer...

And, as Bernice had said, there was no better time of year for it.

Val's younger sisters appeared, dragging their husbands with them through the snow and descending upon their childhood home with whoops of joy and laughter, delight at being all together again. Isabelle found herself the object of three very determined and powerful hugs; the Connor girls had evidently been raised to be unafraid of hard work, and it showed in their embraces – or rather, it was felt. Their enthusiasm and excited questions, the confusion as they interrupted each other and themselves, lifted Isabelle's spirits. She hardly thought of it being Christmas at all.

As the sun neared the horizon and the afternoon slipped on toward evening – Christmas Eve – Isabelle caught herself glancing more and more often toward the kitchen windows. She was only curious about what the weather was doing, she told herself – it had stopped snowing at last, but from the looks of things it could begin again at any moment. That was all she wanted to know: whether it was snowing or not.

But when she spotted the two figures coming across the snowy fields toward the house, she couldn't deny the joyful leap her heart gave. It wasn't the snow at all that she had been watching for, but the stalwart figure of the man she was going to marry. The man who carried a broken heart within him, even as she did – and the surge of light in her heart was the hope that they could heal together.

She threw on her shawl and went to meet them, cheerfully ignoring the cries and teasing of the Connor daughters behind her.

The cold air was sharp to her nose, and she took a deep breath, feeling it all the way into her lungs as she walked through the two-foot-deep snowfall. As she drew closer to the two figures, her steps began to falter; all was not well.

It was Val's voice that she heard first, raised to a pitch she'd never heard before from him, and with a note of anger vibrating deep within, scarcely hidden behind the layer of respect that characterized his speech to his parents.

"And if you hadn't hired that dadgum fool Charley to oversee it, it would have been done a week ago. Why on God's green earth did you bring him back, Pa? You know what happened the last time."

"The job needed to be done, Val, and there wasn't anyone else. You know as well as I do that money is tighter than usual this winter…"

"Because of those three glorious weddings." The bitterness shone through what remained of the respect, and Isabelle flinched.

"That's not the only reason, son. And even if it was, what would you rather I have done? The girls are happy and settled, and I sent them off to start their new families as best as I could."

"I'm not fussing about the weddings, really. It's just frustrating, Pa – when money is so tight, you insist that I stop at home for a week and do nothing. And then bring in Charley Bakey to make a bad situation worse."

"First things must be first, Val. You and Isabelle…"

"I know, Pa."

"You've got to let go of that Linda Mallory. You've got a good girl in front of you, willing to marry you, willing to give you a chance at real happiness. You only need not to be so foolish as to push love away when it comes looking for you. I only hoped that spending time with Isabelle would prove that to you. Any father would do the same. You'll do the same someday yourself."

"I *know*, Pa," Val said again, even more angrily this time. "I know – because a man without a child of his own isn't worth a hill of beans. Isn't that right, Pa?"

Isabelle caught her breath. She suddenly wished she had never come out here to meet them, wished she could trace her steps backwards to keep from hearing the anger in his voice – and the things that they had both said. But they had caught sight of her now, and she saw Val clamp his mouth shut as they walked toward her.

"Well, well, a greeting brigade," said Martin Connor, and she peered at him in the dimming light. Was it just her imagination, or did he look much more tired than usual?

Faded somehow – as though he felt ill. "Did you come to call us in for supper, Isabelle?"

She found her voice at last now that she was forced to it. It was difficult to pretend that she hadn't heard anything that had just happened, but the idea of asking right out what the problem was, or becoming embroiled in it herself, was almost terrifying. She kept her eyes away from Val's, and he in turn did not seek to meet her gaze.

"It's nearly ready," she managed. "Lydia and Ruth and Mary are all here, and their menfolk too."

"Oh, yes? And what did you think of my three little newlywed daughters?"

She smiled at him honestly.

"I like them very much," she said.

Martin chuckled.

"I couldn't hardly expect you to say anything else, considering you're talking to their very proud father," he said, and put his arm around her shoulders, turning her to walk with him toward the house. "I'm proud of all my children, Isabelle – though they have their faults, and even their proud pa isn't blind to them."

She bit her lip, chancing a glance over her shoulder toward Val. But he had his head down.

"I suppose even the best of us are prone to a little mistake now and then," she said. "But that's where love comes in, doesn't it, Martin? Scripture says that love covers over."

Martin nodded, and she was certain now that she wasn't imagining the sadness in his gaze.

"A multitude of sins," he said, and leaned on her a little more heavily as they walked the final few yards to the house.

CHAPTER 7

The ranch was a disaster, and it was all his fault.

It was hard to believe that so much could go wrong in the space of a week. No, not just a week – he had to remind himself of that, as painful as it was to do so. He had stayed away far more than a week. Nearly two, in fact – he had pushed it to the limit, and then beyond. He had felt the call of duty and closed the window to block it out. He had told himself that he was only doing what his father wanted him to do, in spending time with Isabelle Dollenberg, in getting to know her – right up until the moment when it suddenly became a matter of what he wanted to do instead.

He wanted to spend time with her.

He found her company pleasant, soothing, joyful. He felt a lightness of heart when she was around. He let himself be comforted.

And so it was all his fault.

Well, no – part of the blame had to go to his father, and he was willing enough to send it there. They'd had a few rough years on the ranch, though he had hoped that things were evening out at last. Part of the problem, back when his heartache and distraction over Linda Mallory were new, was the hiring of a new hand – Charley Bakey, a local man with a smile constantly at the ready and a wit that lagged behind. He wasn't stupid, not really – but he was easily misled, and thought he was full of bright ideas, despite all evidence to the contrary. Under Charley Bakey's unsteady hand, the ranch had begun to sink like a ship in the storm. It wasn't until Val had managed to pull himself out of his slump for long enough to pitch in again that they had gotten back on something of an even keel.

And now, when he was distracted by something else, Charley had risen again as though from the deeps, clambering aboard the good ship Connor, and hammering holes in the decking.

It wasn't just the tumbledown fencing that should have been repaired a week ago. It wasn't just the fact that half the cows had somehow mysteriously gotten loose from their paddocks. It wasn't even just the fact that Charley had cheerfully brokered a bad deal for eight head of cattle at a loss – and a deal that he had no right to arrange, and eight head of cattle that the ranch could not spare, this close to breeding season. Charley was a walking disaster, as far as Val was concerned, and it absolutely incensed him that his father had so blindly let him back onto the ranch, given him a pitchfork, and told him to go to work.

Yes – that bit was Martin's fault, no doubt about it.

The rest of it, though…

He was morose and silent all through supper that Christmas Eve. He knew that his mood was obvious to all – his sisters knew better than to tease him, but he was the recipient of a barrage of reproachful and disapproving looks from all three of them, as well as his mother. His brothers-in-law, young men that he had grown up with, did their best to trick him into a better attitude, but their best was not good enough. Martin cast him a glance now and then, combining a hopeful smile with a sadness in his eyes that made Val's teeth clench. And Isabelle…

Isabelle alone did not look up at him a single time during supper, let alone speak to him.

He couldn't deny that it hurt. Over the past week and a half, the two of them had begun to forge a friendship – which was far more than he had ever expected to have with this stranger, this mail order bride from Boston, this woman that he was only marrying because his inheritance hung in the balance. But she was sweet, and kind, and thoughtful, and helpful, and pretty – she was a hundred different things that he had not expected, and it hurt that she would not look at him. He couldn't help but wonder whether she might have overheard any of the conversation he'd had with his father on the way back to the house.

For all that, he still resented her, too.

He resented that she had the power to hurt him. He hadn't intended to allow her that, and it felt as though she had taken it without permission. He resented that she might feel hurt, too – when had he ever promised her anything? She was the one who had thrown words like "happiness" and "promise" around willy-nilly, as though words had no consequences.

He resented her because she was not Linda Mallory, and he resented her for being there when Linda Mallory was not, and he resented most of all the fact that his carefully laid plan for the future wasn't working out because his own feelings were getting in the way.

After everything else, that hardly seemed fair, did it?

He sulked his way through supper, and then made his goodnights while everyone else was admiring the tree in the sitting room. His youngest sister, and the nearest to his heart, followed him out afterwards.

"I hope you sleep well, Val," she whispered. "Everything will look brighter in the morning."

He couldn't help but give her a fond smile – though he had to resist the urge to tousle her hair as he had so often done when she was growing up. "You sound awful certain about that, Lydia. I suppose you're wise beyond your years now that you're a married woman."

She smiled at him and went up on her tiptoes to press a kiss to his cheek.

"Nonsense," she said. "It's just Christmas, that's all. That's why I'm certain."

Pondering his family and how things changed, Val took himself to bed.

He could not sleep for a long while, and instead laid awake, staring out the window. The snow clouds had parted, as they so often did in the nighttime, and let the pale moon shine through, bright as a penny. Val thought about his parents, and their great love for each other – he thought about how fragile his father seemed sometimes, and how much Val wished he could take some of the burden off his shoulders, if he would just allow it – he thought of his sisters, and how much he missed them, even though they had driven him so crazy when they were all growing up together.

And finally, he thought of Isabelle, with a sort of wondering regret, and a dawning certainty that things were not as he had expected them to be, at the beginning when he had first written the letter to the agency – and an even more sure certainty that it was all his own fault, somehow.

In the morning, he arose early and went to find his father.

Martin was out in the barn, as he often was before the sun was up, starting the involved process of milking the dairy cows. This early in the morning, and on Christmas Day, no one else was yet up and around. The ranch hands had been given a few days off – and Charley Bakey, Val hoped, had been dismissed entirely. Val wondered listlessly whether his brothers-in-law would think to come and help, as they were staying over for the holidays – but he reckoned they wouldn't. They were town boys, after all, and had never lived on a farm.

Martin looked up from his chore of pouring feed into the trough, an expectant expression on his face. What was it that he wanted from Val? What was it that he was waiting for? Val couldn't be sure, but he wasn't about to let that stop him.

"Well, Pa?"

Martin raised an eyebrow at him.

"Well, Val?"

Val held out for just a few seconds before he couldn't help himself and smiled, shaking his head. His father chuckled.

"You get that stubbornness from your ma, you know."

"Do I? I'm pretty sure she always blames it on you."

"Well, maybe it's from both sides." He tipped another bucket of feed into the trough and clucked to the cows, who moved forward with a few appreciatively lows.

"I'm sorry about the argument last night," Val said. "I shouldn't have lost my temper like I did."

"Oh, I reckon you had a right to be upset. Bringing Charley back wasn't the brightest idea I've ever had. I suppose it was an act of desperation."

"But it didn't need to be," Val said, folding his arms. "If you had just let me keep working..."

"Now, we're not going to have the same argument over again. I won't let your Christmas be ruined entirely. What's done is done. You know my reasons for it, and whether you agree with them or not is up to you. I suppose the only real question is – did it work?"

"Did what work?"

Martin waved his hands briefly in frustration.

"Did you get to know Isabelle? Did you set the date for the wedding? Are you ready to get your life started at last, settle down and start a family?"

Val stared at his father, shaking his head slowly.

"Is that all that really matters to you, Pa? That I settle down and start a family?"

Martin frowned.

"Val – you know how I feel. I understand that things have been tough on you – I understand it better than you might think. But when times are hard, that's when we need to stay strong the most. Now, I want you to be happy. And I know you think that Linda Mallory was your only chance. I'm here to tell you, son, that she wasn't – she isn't – and she never will be. Your future is with the little lady in the house right now, more than likely waking early to help put Christmas breakfast together for a family that isn't even her own. Yet."

Val nodded, watching the play of expressions on his father's face. Earnestness, exhaustion, a wince like a far-off pain – Martin meant every word. But just how did he mean it? Was it really his son's happiness that he cared the most about? Or was it simply a craving for the certainty that his legacy would be passed down, the family name continued?

Not for the first time, Val wondered whether his father cared more about his son – or his unborn grandchildren. The ranch was Martin's pride and joy. The thought of losing it, even after he was gone, must be horrifying.

It was a little painful to try and wrap his mind around – the fact that his father was putting his own legacy ahead of his son's desires for his life. And perhaps he was wrong – but whether he was or not, he had a choice, and a simple one.

Would he do as his father asked, marry Isabelle, and have children to carry on the family name?

Or would he rebel, put his foot down, declare his intent to remain a childless bachelor languishing in his lost love for the rest of his life?

Just how stubborn was he – and was it possible that Martin was even more so?

Martin glanced up at him and grinned.

"You've got that thoughtful look on your face, Val. When you were a boy and looked like that, it meant you were scheming some sort of trouble."

Val smiled back.

"No trouble, Pa," he said. "I promise. Not this time."

After all, what sort of choice was that? He loved his family more than anything in the world, and if his father wanted him to have children, then that was precisely what he would do. Isabelle was a sweet girl and would undoubtedly make a perfectly fine wife. He needn't let his emotions get involved; they could stay tangled up with the lost Linda as much as they liked. But heartbreak didn't need to get in his way. He could marry, pass down the family name, inherit the ranch, and save it from disaster.

After all, he inherited stubbornness from both sides. Nothing would stop him from what he needed to do.

CHAPTER 8

Christmas came and went. The tree was much admired; everyone ate until they were stuffed, and then ate some more regardless; the presents were opened; and thanks were given. Val threw himself into enjoying the time spent with his family. He felt as though a new understanding had grown between himself and Isabelle. Their relationship was clear cut, now – not fuzzy and confusing, as it had been. He could smile at her without it reaching his eyes, speak to her without unnecessary warmth, and spend time with her without allowing her to take over his every thought. She would be his wife and the mother of his children, and nothing more. And that was enough.

That was more than enough.

And if his dreaming brain had other ideas – if Isabelle seemed to creep into every dream he had, in fact – that was no one's business but his own.

Two days after Christmas, on December the 27th, the sisters that were formerly the Connor girls packed up their bags and their husbands and said their goodbyes. Val walked out after them, watching the wagons disappear into the foggy day, and turned to see Isabelle waiting for him by the gate, patiently, wrapped up against the cold.

"They're very sweet, your sisters," she said as he came up to her. She offered him a smile. "Of course, that's only to be expected, considering who their parents are."

"They've turned out well, it's true."

"And they seem to be very happy."

"They do."

She hesitated for a moment, and he glanced at her swiftly, then just as quickly away. It was clear that she had something she wanted to say – and with a sinking feeling, he wasn't entirely sure whether he wanted to hear it.

"Val – do you think we will be as happy as they are?"

He raised an eyebrow.

"What a question," he murmured. "Why do you ask that, Isabelle?"

"Because – well – it seemed a few days ago that you and I were getting along quite well. Very well, in fact. I thought – we seemed to be friends. But after I heard your discussion with your father…"

"What?" he said sharply, raising his head to stare at her.

She bit her lip.

"I didn't intend to – it was just that I was coming out to meet you, and I caught a few words."

"I see. Well, that was between my father and me. Nothing to do with you."

"I know – I'm sorry. I just…" She twisted her fingers together and looked so unhappy that he couldn't help but feel sorry for speaking to her so harshly. Without quite intending to, he reached out and put a hand over hers, drawing them into his palm, closing his fingers around hers. She looked down at their joined hands for a moment and seemed to steady herself. "I started to worry that perhaps marriage isn't what you really want. You know that I have…a tragedy in my past, and I know that you do as well. Val, I don't want to be married…"

His eyes flew wide, searching hers.

"What?"

"I mean...I don't want to be married if I can't make you happy. That's all I want. To make you happy – for that may mean that I have some chance at happiness myself."

For a moment, his resolve faltered as his heart clenched within him, and his emotions welled up in his throat, fighting to be spoken aloud. He held onto her hands as though they were a lifeline and got control of himself slowly. *Remember, Percival Connor, that you're only marrying her to beget an heir...*

"Happiness isn't the main object of a marriage," he said, hating how stiff and formal he sounded. "And you're right – I'm not getting married to you because I want to be happy."

Her eyes opened wide, fixed on his. There was something like fear, something like sadness deep within them.

"Then..."

"My father wants me to marry and have children to pass on the family name – and the ranch. That's all that matters. Anything apart from that is simply an afterthought – whether we're happy or not."

Now her eyes were filling with tears, and he tilted his head curiously, not understanding where this wash of emotion was coming from.

"That's – that's all that matters?"

"It's the main thing," he repeated. "I won't try to make you unhappy, Isabelle, don't think that – I think we get on very well. But it doesn't really matter whether we love each other or not, in my opinion. It doesn't really matter whether you're a good wife, though I appreciate that you intend to try to be one, and I believe you will be. That's all besides the point. The main thing – the only thing – is to make sure that there are more Connors around to inherit the ranch."

Isabelle made a small sound, as though there were something in her throat, and she couldn't quite breathe.

"And if I couldn't have children," she managed. "What then?"

Val's heart shuddered, but he kept his voice as steady as he could.

"Then I couldn't marry you," he said. "I can't marry someone who can't give me children. That's all."

She nodded and turned away from him. Try though he might to keep hold of her hands, her fingers slipped through his grasp, and she walked away, back toward the house.

"But you can," he called after her, feeling suddenly desperate. "There's no need to worry about it, Isabelle – everything's going to be just fine. You and me, Isabelle, we're going to get married – soon – after the first of the year."

But her head stayed down, and she didn't slow, or stop, or look around.

Val stayed where he was for a long while, watching the quiet ranch house, trying to picture it with children racing around it, as it had been when he and his sisters were young. But he couldn't see anyone there. It was as though it were empty – empty of everyone, even Isabelle.

CHAPTER 9

"Val? Have you seen Isabelle?"

Val stomped the frozen snow from his boots before he entered the kitchen, knowing that his mother hated it when anything was tracked in – and that Agnes was still on holidays, and thus not available to clean up the floor.

"Not since last night. I think she had a headache and went to bed early."

"I haven't seen her this morning." Bernice twisted her hands together, her face drawn with worry. "She's usually up before me. Do you suppose she still isn't feeling well? Poor thing."

Val put a hand on his mother's shoulder comfortingly.

"I'll go up and knock on her door," he said. "I'm sure everything will be just fine."

As he mounted the stairs, his own words came back to him, an echo of what he had called after Isabelle as she walked away from him the night before. He paused for a moment at the top of the stairs, gathering his thoughts. It felt as though he owed her an apology – though he wasn't entirely sure what for. Something had changed between them, that much was certain. But he would make it right – whatever it was.

He paused just outside her door, raising his hand, with the realization that the door was ajar.

"Isabelle?"

Nothing but silence.

Holding his breath, feeling as though something huge and terrible were rushing toward him, he pushed the door open tentatively. Still nothing, not a single sound – no cry of protest or surprise, no morning greeting, not even the sound of her breath or of movement. He pushed the door all the way open and took in the scene. A quiet, still room, looking just as it had a few weeks before when she had first arrived, and he had carried her bag upstairs for her. It looked as though it hadn't been inhabited for years, as though she had never been there at all.

Her bag was missing; the bed looked as though it hadn't been slept in; everything had a forlorn tinge to it, as though it had been left behind. The only thing out of place was the small, folded piece of paper in the middle of the counterpane.

With slightly trembling hands, he stepped forward and reached for it.

He was still staring at it, hardly comprehending what he was reading, when he heard his mother's footsteps coming up the stairs, followed by the heavier tread of his father.

"Val?"

"Val, is something wrong?"

He turned to them, and his mother put a hand to her mouth at the sight of him, her eyes fixed on his with worry and love.

"Oh, my dear – you're crying."

Val swiped at his eyes with the back of his hand.

"I'm not," he declared. "I'm not. Look, Ma – see for yourself."

He handed the letter over to her, and she held it up to read aloud.

My dear Val –

I'm so very sorry that things must be this way. I can only hope that this will not hurt you in the slightest; I know better by now than to expect that you might feel the same way that I do, but knowing also that you understand the pain of rejection, I hope that this does not bring back any bad memories. This letter is the best that I can do by way of explanation. I could not bear to have to tell you face to face.

So often over the past few weeks, I have yearned to share my final secret with you. You've been so kind, kinder than I had any expectation of, and what your pa told me about you the very first day I arrived is true: you're a good man, a gentleman. I believe there isn't a better in all of Missouri, if not America entirely. I only wish that I had been worthy of winning your love and the chance to make you happy as your wife.

But that privilege is not to be mine.

You know my history – some of it, at least. The tragic passing of my husband, a day after Christmas last year. It seems so impossible that it has been a whole year since I last saw Thomas – and even more impossible that it hasn't been a decade at least. I have spent so much of the past year in tears, in mourning and sorrow, and when I made up my mind to marry again it was with the reluctant realization that I could not let my life just stop at twenty-three. Thomas would not have wanted that for me. He loved me – he would want me to love again.

I was determined to do my best – and I believe that I have succeeded, on that count at least.

You see, I'm afraid that I do love you. Truly and deeply – and I say that I am afraid because I know you cannot love me back. Perhaps even that would be bearable were it not for that final secret – the knowledge I bear, that I haven't been able to put words to until now. I must take your hope and dash it.

Your dearest wish and fondest hope – to have children with your new wife.

The truth is that it wasn't just my husband that I lost last year. I told you the story of why I am afraid of heights – what I did not tell you is that, at the time when I fell, I was expecting. I was gravely injured, and for a week my life hung in the balance. When I awoke from my long illness, it was to find that the child Thomas and I had been so sweetly awaiting was no more. And more than that – the doctor who attended me said that I would not be able to bear another.

It broke my heart then, though Thomas comforted me as best as he could. Every woman wants to be a mother; every wife wants to give her husband children. It breaks my heart again now to know that I must leave you and break our engagement because of my own failing. The only comfort I have is in knowing that a man as good and kind as you will easily find another woman to love you and marry you – though selfishly I doubt that she will ever love you as you deserve – or as much as I do.

I do, and I will – forever, Val, no matter what comes next.

I hereby free you from your engagement to me and wish you all the happiness that I could never bring you.

Yours ever,

Isabelle

In the silence that fell over the little spare room after the letter was read, Martin Connor drew in a deep breath.

"Val," he said, his voice nearing a groan. "Oh, my son…"

Val's eyes flew to him, widening with alarm. His father put a hand to his heart, and Val leapt forward, taking Martin's arm, leading him to the bed.

"Sit down, Pa. What's wrong?"

Martin shook his head.

"Oh, Martin." Bernice fussed around him, straightening his collar ineffectually and smoothing her hand over his gray hair. "What is it? Is it your heart again?"

Val turned sharp eyes on his mother.

"Again?" he said. "What do you mean, Ma?"

Martin shook his head.

"No – no, Bernice, don't worry. It's not my heart – it's just regret that stabs me through, now. Val, that poor girl. She must have walked into town early this morning when you and I were in the barn. She must be heartbroken, and after she's already had too much heartbreak for one young woman to bear." He pushed at Val's shoulder. "What are you doing here? Go after her."

Val shook his head stubbornly.

"No," he said. "Not yet. Not until you explain something to me – what's this about your heart acting up?"

Martin sighed and exchanged glances with his wife.

"It's been a little while now," he said.

"Eleven months," Bernice said quietly. "Eleven months and two weeks, precisely."

Val put a hand to his forehead.

"You never said…"

"You were so busy with your own heartbreak, we didn't want to worry you," Martin said. "Besides, the doctor wasn't too concerned at the time."

"At the time?"

"Well, he's had some time to think it over, I reckon."

"The truth of the matter is, your father's heart is not in very good condition," said Bernice, taking her husband's hand and holding it fast.

"No surprise there," Martin said. "It ain't exactly new."

"There isn't much to be done about it now. All we can do is live in hope."

Val shook his head.

"Hope is an awful uncomfortable place to set up house," he said.

"It's better than the alternative," his mother said crisply. "Well, now, you know the truth of that. Your father is meant to get plenty of rest and avoid stressing himself as much as he can – which is more difficult than it should be, it seems."

"Never mind that," Martin said. "My heart's just fine now, Val. Go on with you, go and fetch Isabelle back. That poor girl."

But Val shook his head again, adamantly.

"I can't," he said. "You heard what she wrote yourself. She can't have children – and that's all you want, Pa, is for me to have young uns and pass down the family name, make sure that Connor Ranch stays that way."

For a long, quiet moment, his father gazed at him. Finally, he shook his head and heaved a sigh, putting a hand on Val's shoulder.

"I did wrong by you," he said softly. "I let you think that it was all that mattered to me – to anyone. And it's my own fault, I admit it. I worry about the future, Val – I worry about what will happen to the ranch. We're in debt, more than I like to think about. Most of all I worry about your ma." He reached up with his free hand, cupping Bernice's cheek, and they smiled at each other, eyes aglow with their long-lasting love. "I wanted to make sure she was cared for, when something happened to me."

"Pa, I would never let anything happen to Ma."

"I know you would intend to take care of her. But the way you've been wrapped up in your sorrow this past year and a half, Val – the way it's eaten you up inside… No one can blame you for it, but I couldn't let things stand as they were.

I thought you needed to marry to move on. That's the reason I told you I would withhold the inheritance until you married and had a child – but I was wrong, and I'm sorry. Boy, nothing would stop me from handing this ranch down to you, my only son. I'm so proud of you, and everything you've become." His sparkling eyes were swimming a little, Val saw. He felt his own heart touched by a warm hand, as though he were a little boy again and his father had taken him into his arms. "It doesn't matter to me whether you have children or not. What matters is that you're happy – and that girl was bound and determined to make sure that you were."

"But I don't love her," said Val. "I like her, it's true – but she was right when she said that my feelings aren't the same as hers."

His father eyed him keenly.

"Is that so, son?"

"That's so."

"Because it looks to me like you're crying again."

With a sense of wonder, Val touched his fingertips to his cheek. They came away wet. He looked up at his parents, eyes wide.

"You think I…"

"I know it," said his mother. "I saw it the moment you two met. You've been clinging on to that Linda Mallory all along, but she's nothing but a bad habit. Isabelle Dollenberg is the girl for you, my only son – and you'd better hasten to Culver's Creek if you want to stop her from slipping through your fingers."

Val was on his feet before he even realized it. He paused at the doorway and turned back to them, shaking his head.

"If she can't have children," he said, "then there won't be anyone to pass the ranch down to. We'll lose it from the family in the end. Connor Ranch – won't be Connor Ranch."

His father shook his head back, and grinned.

"I reckon there are ways around that," he said. "Why, there's an orphanage over in Cahill that's practically bursting at the seams. I reckon you two should adopt twins – a little boy and a little girl. Just to start out with, I mean."

Val turned his eyes to his mother, who smiled at him, the love in her heart shining in her eyes.

"Go on, Percival Connor," she said. "You've got a wedding to plan."

CHAPTER 10

For the second time that month, Isabelle Dollenberg stood on the station platform at Culver's Creek, Missouri.

But how different it was this time.

When she had arrived, scarcely three weeks before, she had been full of hope. Hope that things would turn out for the best – hope that she could be the answer to a prayer, and hope that her own prayer would be answered in turn. She had left everything behind, including the memories of the life she'd once led with Thomas Dollenberg, and yet so much had been waiting for her just ahead…

Now…there was nothing.

She had no new life to go to. No old life to return to. Nothing but an aching head and an aching heart, full of lovelorn wanting, full to the brim of sadness and regret – but something like satisfaction, too, for she believed she was doing the right thing.

She had promised Val Connor that she would make him happy.

If he could have children, it would secure his happiness – even if leaving him behind meant that her heart broke in two once more.

She was trying to get control of herself and stop her tears from continuing when she heard a familiar voice behind her.

"I see that you're no longer enjoying the hospitality of the Connors, eh? I told you, miss, I'd be more than happy to see to it that you were taken care of."

Her heart leapt into her throat, and she turned to find the kindly, middle-aged face of Teller Smith, the first person to welcome her into Culver's Creek all those days ago when she had arrived. She managed a smile that she did not feel.

"Hello again," she said. "No need to worry about me, Mr. Smith. I'm perfectly fine. Just waiting."

He glanced up at the skies.

"Perfectly fine, miss? It's snowing."

"I know it."

"You ought to wait inside, is what I think. Come on, I'll take you to the dining hall at the inn and buy you a cup of coffee. Maybe a little jot of whiskey in it wouldn't go amiss on a day like this. Come on," he cajoled her. "It's Christmas."

She shook her head.

"Not anymore," she said. "It's nearly the new year."

You and me, Isabelle – we're going to be married, soon, after the first of the year...

She shook the ghost of Val's words from her mind and refocused on Teller Smith, who was still smiling at her as though he expected her to capitulate at any moment.

"Close enough, eh?" he said. "Still worth a cup of coffee, anyhow. Besides, miss – what exactly is it you're waiting for?"

"Me, I think."

Isabelle's heart leapt higher, beating wildly, as though it were about to sprout wings and fly away. She had been so caught up with Teller Smith that she hadn't even seen the other man step onto the platform. But there he was, tall, broad-shouldered, the most handsome man she'd ever seen before in her life.

"Val," she whispered.

He stepped past Teller Smith, who knew when he was beaten and withdrew without another word. Val took off his hat, and a few snowflakes settled immediately in his black hair.

"I'm sorry," he said. "I'm sorry."

She raised a trembling hand, and he took it in his, holding it comfortingly.

"What are you doing here?"

"I read your letter."

"I know you must have – what are you doing here?"

He tilted his head, smiling down at her.

"I came to make a promise," he said.

"A promise?"

"A promise – as best as I can. Let's see, how did it go?" He looked thoughtful for a moment, as though pulling the words from his memory. "I intend to be the best husband I can be to you – and do everything I can to make…ah, yes. To make our future a happy one." He pulled her a step closer. "Don't leave, Isabelle. You do make me happy – even now, before we're married. I know what heartbreak feels like. I don't want to feel it ever again."

"But – but – I can't…give you children…"

He leaned his forehead against hers, closing his eyes.

"If you can give me *you*," he said, "that's the most any man could ever hope for. I told you before, Isabelle, and I meant it – everything will turn out just fine. You and me, Isabelle Dollenberg – we can face anything, as long as we're together. You just have to trust me."

She lifted her head away from his and wiped away her tears, half laughing.

"I – I don't know what to say."

"Well, I'll tell you what my pa told me, not too long ago. Don't be so foolish as to push love away when it comes looking for you." He grinned down at her and spoke softly. "And here I am."

He spread his arms wide, and she walked into them, letting out a sigh of relief. At last, at last – she was home.

Well – not quite.

"You're freezing," he whispered into her ear.

She laughed.

"It's snowing," she reminded him.

"Ah, yes. Tell you what – why don't we follow Teller's suggestion and go to the dining hall at the inn? A cup of coffee would be good right about now, warm the hands." He pressed a kiss to her forehead and stepped back, smiling. "And the heart. Besides, you and me – we've got some things to plan."

She arched an eyebrow at him.

"Oh, yes?"

"Oh, yes," he repeated back. "A wedding, for example…and what to name the children."

She stared at him in wide eyed wonder, and he threw back his head and laughed.

"Come on, Isabelle," he said, taking her by the hand. "Come with me, if you want to find out what comes next."

She held on tightly and went with him.

The End

CONTINUE READING...

Thank you for reading *The Deserted Groom!* Are you wondering **what to read next?** Why not read *The Brother Takes the Bride?* **Here's a peek for you:**

The wintry sun was sinking low in the near-white skies as Andrew Martin whistled the dogs up and closed the fence behind the last of the cattle. Even in his leather gloves, his hands were cracking from the dry cold; he pulled them out and rubbed them together, blowing on them to try and get some warmth going. It was mid-February, and it had been a long, hard winter from the onset of November; storm had followed storm, dumping several feet of snow on the little family ranch in Culver's Creek, Missouri. The storm clouds had gone on their way two weeks ago, leaving below-zero temperatures and frozen drifts of snow behind to mark their memory.

Spring couldn't come quickly enough, in his opinion. He could do with a bit of good weather.

With the ranch dogs gamboling at his heels, he trudged through the frozen snow toward the long, low ranch house, noting absently that it was badly in need of a new coat of paint. Whitewash would do. As soon as there was some warmth in the world. It was a big job to tackle on his own, but with a wry candidness, he admitted to himself that it was too much to hope that anyone would be ready and able to help him. His ma was too arthritic to hold a brush for longer than a few minutes at a time; and as for Clint, well...

It wasn't that Clinton Martin was unwilling to help around the ranch. Granted, he had made it clear years ago that he had no interest in being a rancher himself, but as long as Andrew didn't require him to help herd the cattle, he was willing enough to help out with other chores. And he lived in the ranch house, too – though it didn't seem to pain him to see it grow dilapidated, as it pained Andrew. Andrew had always been the one to take pride in the family homestead. Clint always had his sights set elsewhere.

But that was neither here nor there. No, Clint's problem wasn't unwillingness to help. These days, the problem lay more in his absence than anything else. He left before breakfast most mornings, and often arrived well after dark, missing a hot supper, though he seemed content with a warmed-over plate.

Visit HERE To Read More!

https://ticahousepublishing.com/mail-order-brides.html

THANKS FOR READING!

If you **love Mail Order Bride Romance, <u>Visit Here</u>**

https://wesrom.subscribemenow.com/

to find out about all **<u>New Susannah Calloway Romance</u> <u>Releases!</u> We will let you know as soon as they become available!**

If you enjoyed *The Deserted Groom,* would you kindly take a couple minutes to leave a positive review on Amazon? It only takes a moment, and positive reviews truly make a difference. Thank you so much! I appreciate it!

Turn the page to discover more Mail Order Bride Romances just for you!

MORE MAIL ORDER BRIDE ROMANCES FOR YOU!

We love clean, sweet, adventurous Mail Order Bride Romances and have a lovely library of Susannah Calloway titles just for you!

Box Sets — A Wonderful Bargain for You!

https://ticahousepublishing.com/bargains-mob-box-sets.html

Or enjoy Susannah's single titles. You're sure to find many favorites! (Remember all of them can be downloaded FREE with Kindle Unlimited!)

Sweet Mail Order Bride Romances!

https://ticahousepublishing.com/mail-order-brides.html

ABOUT THE AUTHOR

Susannah has always been intrigued with the Western movement - prairie days, mail-order brides, the gold rush, frontier life! As a writer, she's excited to combine her love of story with her love of all that is Western. Presently, Susannah lives in Wyoming with her hubby and their three amazing children.

www.ticahousepublishing.com
contact@ticahousepublishing.com

Made in United States
Troutdale, OR
06/27/2023